W9-CPF-123

How Do I Love You?

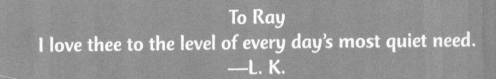

To Ray
I love thee to the level of every day's most quiet need.
—L. K.

To Emiline
—L. M.

No part of this publication may be reproduced, stored in a retrieval system,
or transmitted in any form or by any means, electronic, mechanical, photocopying,
recording, or otherwise, without written permission of the publisher. For information
regarding permission, write to HarperCollins Children's Books, a division of HarperCollins
Publishers, 1350 Avenue of the Americas, New York, NY 10019.

ISBN-13: 978-0-439-02717-5
ISBN-10: 0-439-02717-9

Text copyright © 2006 by Leslie Kimmelman.
Illustrations copyright © 2006 by Lisa McCue. All rights reserved.
Published by Scholastic Inc., 557 Broadway, New York, NY 10012, by arrangement with
HarperCollins Children's Books, a division of HarperCollins Publishers. SCHOLASTIC and
associated logos are trademarks and/or registered trademarks of Scholastic Inc.

12 11 10 9 8 7 6 5 4 3 2 1   7 8 9 10 11 12/0

Printed in the U.S.A.   08

First Scholastic printing, February 2007

Typography by Amelia May Anderson

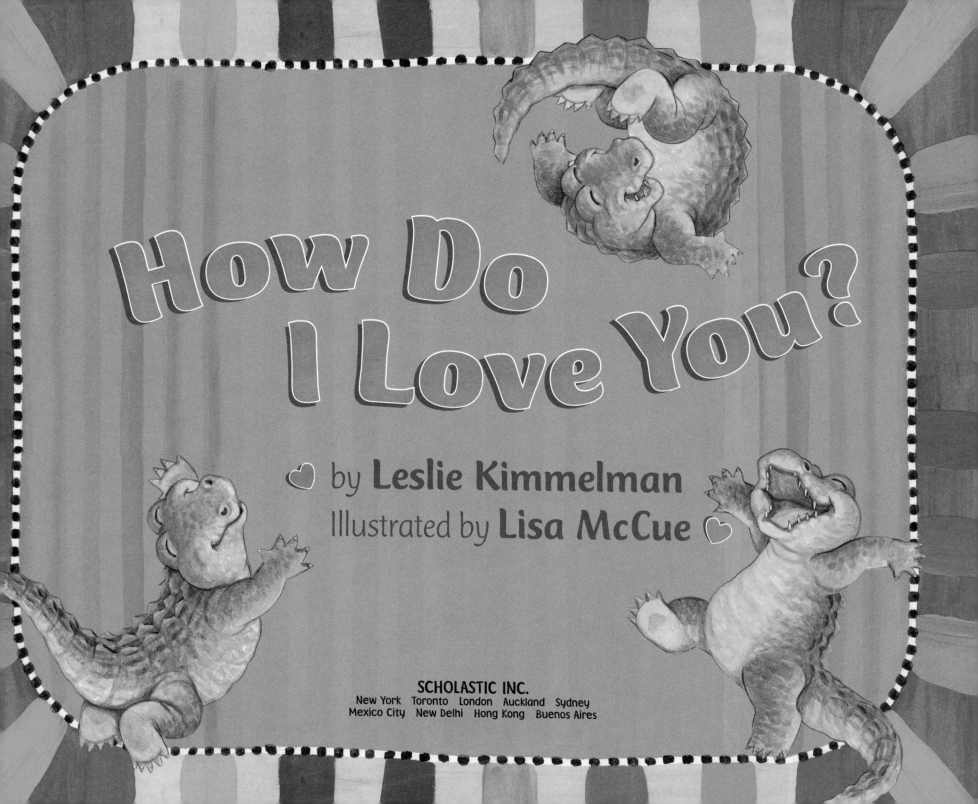

How Do I Love You?

♡ by **Leslie Kimmelman**

Illustrated by **Lisa McCue** ♡

SCHOLASTIC INC.
New York   Toronto   London   Auckland   Sydney
Mexico City   New Delhi   Hong Kong   Buenos Aires

How do I love you, little one?
Let me count the ways. . . .

One in sunshine;

Two in snow;

Three on rainy days.

Four I love you right side up,

Five and upside down.

Six I love your happy smile;

I even love your frown.

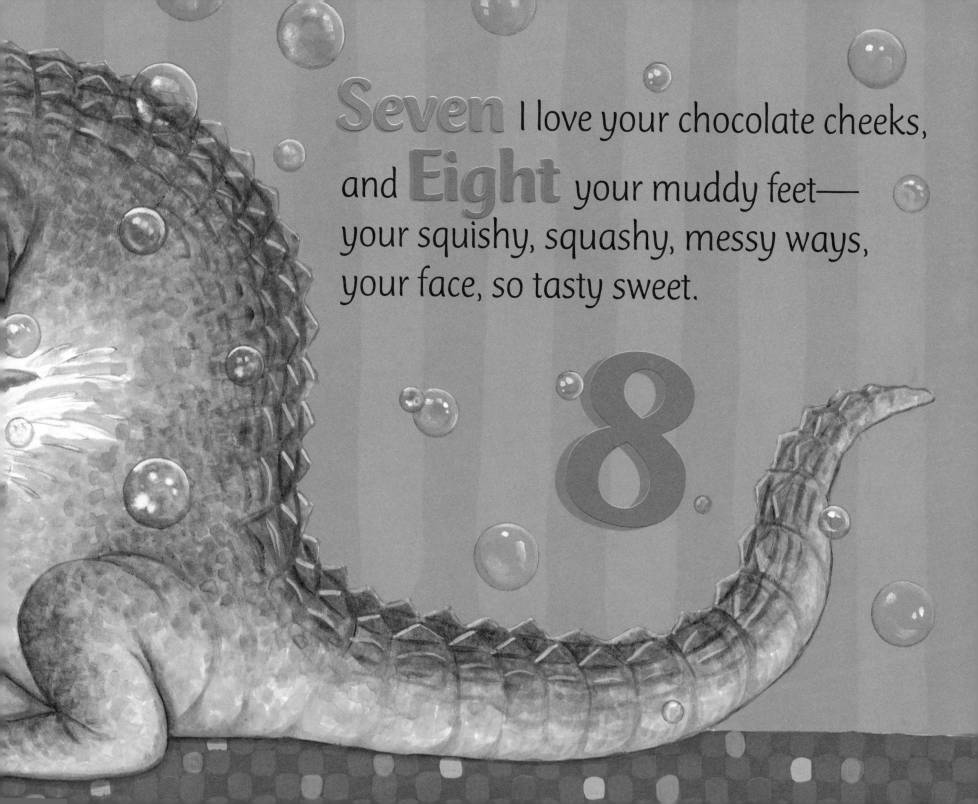

Seven I love your chocolate cheeks,
and **Eight** your muddy feet—
your squishy, squashy, messy ways,
your face, so tasty sweet.

8

Nine I love when we jump waves
each summer at the shore;
and search for seashells—that makes **Ten**.

10

Let's count a little more.

Eleven

I love your pictures;
I hang them on the wall.

Twelve I'll love you when you're grown;

Thirteen I love you small.

14
Fourteen
Fifteen
Sixteen
15

each silly dance you do,
or spin you spin, or grin you grin
when you try something new.

17

I love you morning, noon, and night—
that's number **Seventeen**:

in summer, autumn, winter, spring,
and each day in between.

Eighteen I love you 'neath the moon that shines when day is done,

18

Nineteen and more than all the stars— I can't count every one.

19

I really love to count with you,
and up to Twenty's tough.
But when it comes to loving you,
well, twenty's not enough.

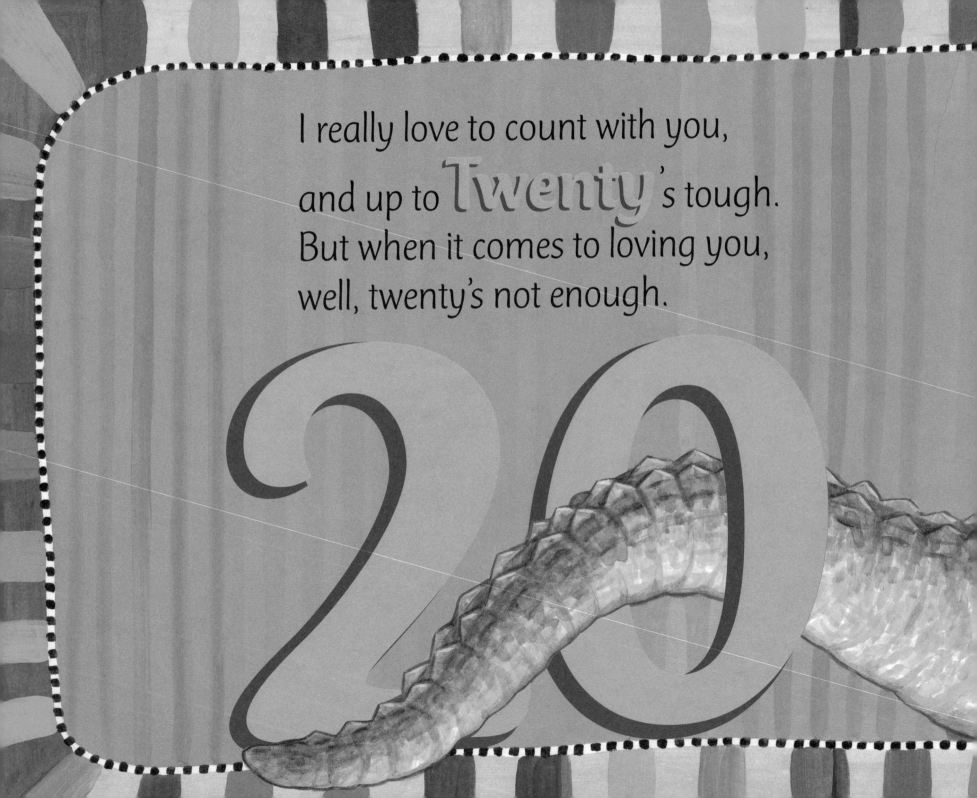